Ladybugs DO NOT Go to Pre-School

Ali Rutstein   Niña Nill

Bright Light

Hardie Grant Children's Publishing

To Sam, the original ladybug – AR

For my son, Elijah – NN

Hardie Grant acknowledges the Traditional Owners of the Country on which we work, the Wurundjeri People of the Kulin Nation and the Gadigal People of the Eora Nation, and recognizes their continuing connection to the land, waters and culture. We pay our respects to their Elders past and present.

Bright Light
an imprint of Hardie Grant Children's Publishing
Wurundjeri Country
Ground Floor, Building 1, 658 Church Street
Richmond, Victoria 3121, Australia
Melbourne | Sydney | London | San Francisco
www.hardiegrantchildrens.com

ISBN: 9781761213472
First published in Australia in 2023
This edition published in 2024

Publisher Chren Byng **Design** Pooja Desai
Editorial Joanna Wong with Johanna Gogos **Production** Sally Davis

The paper this book is printed on is from FSC®-certified forests and other sources. FSC® promotes environmentally responsible, socially beneficial and economically viable management of the world's forests.

Ravi stretched his legs, wiggled his antennae and scuttled downstairs.

'Morning, sleepy head,' said Mom. 'Your cornflakes are on the table.'

Ravi frowned. 'Ladybugs don't eat cornflakes.'

Mom looked up. 'Did I say cornflakes? Silly me. I meant aphids.'

Ravi eyed his bowl suspiciously, then swallowed a spoonful.

Hmm, he preferred his aphids a little less soggy.
But he *slurped* his bowl clean.

After all, Ravi was a hungry sort of ladybug.

'Come on,' said Mom. 'Let's get ready for preschool. We don't want to be late on your first day.'

But Ravi did not come on.

He folded his legs. 'Ladybugs don't go to preschool.'

Then he *zoomed* into the garden
to search for some fresh, *crunchy*
aphids, his bright wings flapping
bravely in the breeze.

'Brrr!' Mom shivered. 'Ravi, here's your sweater.'

'Ladybugs don't wear sweaters,' Ravi replied.

'They do when it's chilly,' said Mom. 'Otherwise,
they get little icicles on their wing cases.'

Ravi knew this was untrue, but *all* his
legs had goose bumps.

So, he got dressed, taking care not to squash
his antennae or wrinkle his wings.

'Time for teeth!' said Mom.

'Ladybugs don't have teeth ... but my mandibles could do with a clean – they're full of aphid guts.'

Ravi showed Mom his *ooey, gooey* mandibles.

'Oof! Disgusting!' said Mom, laughing.

Ravi brushed his mandibles until they were sparkly. He grinned at Mom.

'Beautiful! Let's go!'

Ravi stopped smiling.

'I think I might stay home today
and crawl around the veggie garden
instead,' he said in a small voice.

Mom stroked Ravi's wings. 'You'll like preschool, Ravi. There'll be new friends to meet, and I'm sure you'll get to do lots of painting!'

Ravi fiddled with his antennae. 'OK,' he said.

After all, Ravi was an artistic sort of ladybug.

'But only if I can have aphid juice
in my water bottle and ... we *FLY* there!'

On the way, Ravi stopped
to chat with friends.

Snaffled a quick snack.

And inspected *lot*s of interesting things.

After all, Ravi was a curious sort of ladybug.

As they turned the corner to preschool, Ravi hung back.

Beneath his exoskeleton, his insides squirmed and churned.

'I want to go home,' he whispered.
'I'm absolutely sure ladybugs do *not* go to preschool.'

'I'll stay for a few minutes to check if they do,' Mom whispered back.

Ravi took some deep breaths.

He smoothed his wings, and remembered that ladybugs might be small, but their bright colours made them brave.

'I think the flower beds might be a good spot for ladybugs,' said Ravi.

'Mom, look! Ladybugs really
do go to preschool!'

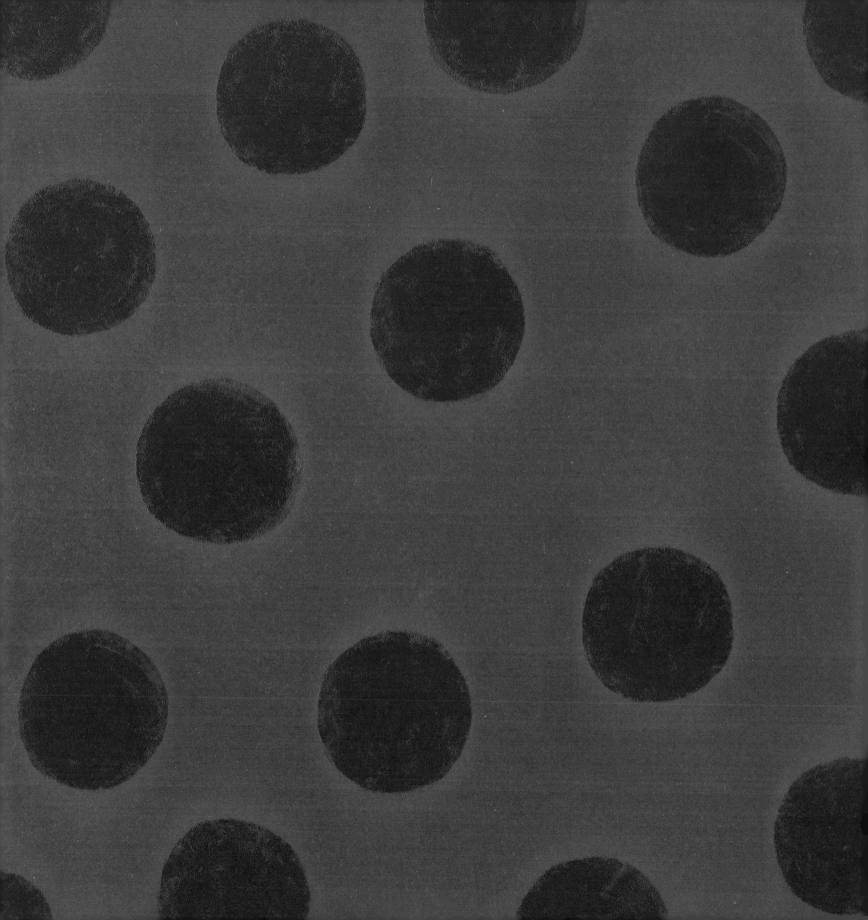